One WORD Pearl

written
by
Nicole Groeneweg

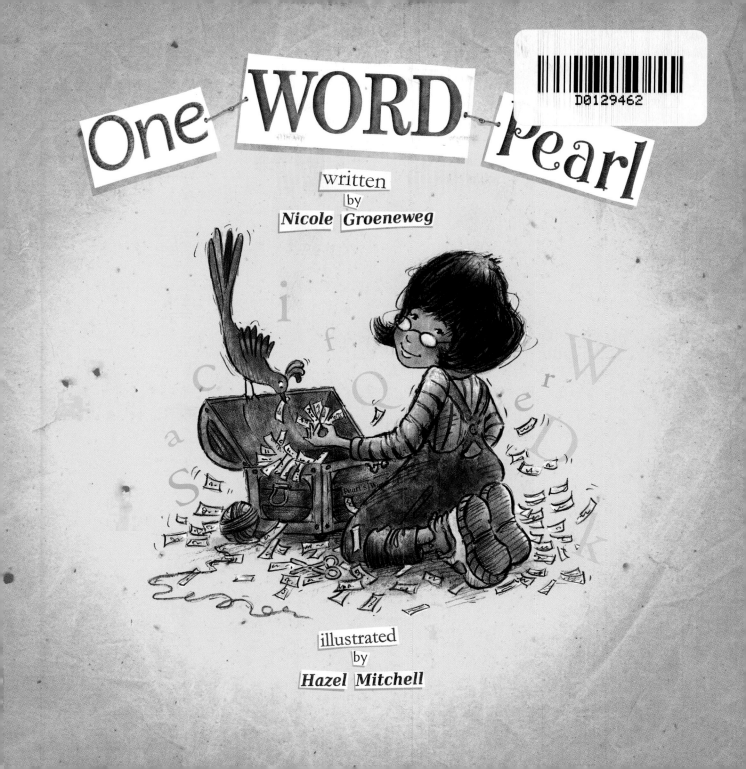

illustrated
by
Hazel Mitchell

To those who taught me to love words:
my family, my students, and the 'Ever Afters'   —*Nicole Groeneweg*

To Nancy, a good friend   —*Hazel Mitchell*

Established in 1921, the National Association of Elementary School Principals (NAESP) leads in the advocacy and support for elementary- and middle-level principals in the United States, Canada and overseas. The NAESP Foundation, founded in 1982, is the charitable arm of NAESP and is dedicated to securing and stewarding private gifts and grants that benefit NAESP.

One Word Pearl
Text Copyright © 2013 Nicole Groeneweg
Illustration Copyright © 2013 Hazel Mitchell

A Mackinac Island Book
Published by Charlesbridge
85 Main Street
Watertown, MA 02472
(617) 926-0329
www.charlesbridge.com

Library of Congress Cataloging-in-Publication Data
Groeneweg, Nicole.
One word Pearl / by Nicole Groeneweg ; [illustrations by Hazel Mitchell].
  p. cm.
  Summary: Pearl loves words, and stores them in a treasure chest at home but one day she opens her chest and finds that all the words are gone, and she no longer has the answers at school.
  ISBN 978-1-934133-53-8 (reinforced for library use)
  ISBN 978-1-934133-54-5 (softcover)
  ISBN 978-1-60734-672-2 (ebook pdf)
1. Vocabulary—Juvenile fiction. 2. Communication—Juvenile fiction. 3. Self-confidence—Juvenile fiction. [1. Vocabulary—Fiction. 2. Communication—Fiction. 3. Self-confidence—Fiction.] I. Mitchell, Hazel, ill. II. Title.
PZ7.G89248One 2013
813.6—dc23   2013009763

Packaged by Blue Tree Creative, LLC.
www.bluetreecreative.com

Printed by 1010 Printing International Limited in China
(hc) 10 9 8 7 6 5 4 3 2 1
(sc) 10 9 8 7 6 5 4 3

Mackinac Island Press
for the love of reading

Words Words Words

Pearl loved words. She collected words.
She pasted words all over her room.
She even strung words together
like beads on a necklace
and stored them in a
treasure chest.

Pearl's Word Chest

Luxury Photo! MAYHEM

One morning Pearl looked at all her wonderful words. She thought of words that would tell stories, words that would sing songs, and words that would make poems rhyme.

She thought and thought and soon the words began to

SPIN and roll and *twist* and **turn**.

A *tornado* of words **whirled** around Pearl! *rushing* wind.

So many words. So *fast* she couldn't think. She grabbed her word chest and escaped the

Outside her room, safe from the storm, Pearl opened her chest. But the wind had only left a handful of words—not enough to tell a story, not enough to sing a song, and not enough to make a poem rhyme.

So Pearl decided she would use only one precious word at a time.

When she went to school on Monday, she *twirled* and spoke in **swirly, curly, whirly** words.

One word at a time.

Her teacher and friends called her **One Word Pearl**.

When her teacher said, "Name something round," Pearl answered, **Pinwheels.**

When her friend Jack asked her what she had for lunch, Pearl said, **Jellyrolls.**

And when Molly showed her a picture of worms, Pearl giggled and said, *Squiggles!*

On Tuesday Pearl **hopped** to school and spoke in

hoppity,   POPPITY

floppity,   words.

When her teacher said, "Pearl, name
something you wear,"
Pearl answered,

FLIPFLOPS.

When Jack asked what
she had for snack,
Pearl said, **Popcorn**.

And when Molly showed
her a scribble picture,
Pearl laughed and said,

Sloppy!

On Wednesday Pearl SKIPPED to school and spoke in skippity, pippity, flippity words.

When her teacher said, "Name something rain does," Pearl answered, **Drips.**

When Jack asked what she had in her lunchbox, Pearl said, **CHIPS.**

And when Molly showed her a picture of the moon hiding, Pearl said, *Eclipse!*

On Thursday Pearl spoke in frilly, thrilly, silly, words.

When her teacher said, "Name a breed of dog," Pearl answered,

Poodles.

When Jack asked, "What can you trade?" Pearl said,

Noodles.

But when Molly showed Pearl her notebook, Pearl smiled,

Doodles!

Friday was **pizzazz** day!
Every word Pearl used *sizzled!*

She used words like bedazzled,

JAZZIEST

and DAZZLING.

**One word
at a time.**

Each word rolled off her
tongue like a **BUBBLE**
in a *fizzy* drink.

It was Pearl's
snazziest
day of the week.

The next day was Saturday and when Pearl opened her word chest, it was empty.

Not **ONE** word left.

Not **ONE** word to tickle her tongue.

So Pearl decided she wouldn't use any words. She'd be known as *No Word Pearl!*

On Monday when her teacher asked her to name her favorite word, Pearl stuttered but had nothing to say.

When Jack asked what she had for lunch, Pearl hung her head and slinked away.

And when Molly showed her a self-portrait, Pearl smiled,

but only halfway.

The teacher tried again, but Pearl did not speak
—not one word all day.

No more razzamatazz.

No more jiggamajazz.

No more sizzling words.

NO WORDS AT ALL.

Pearl's words were gone.
She was *No Word Pearl* all week.

The next Saturday Pearl peeked
in her word chest again.

Still empty.

Pearl knew she had
to tackle the
word tornado
in her room.

So she faced her fears and opened the door. And . . .

. . . she saw words. Words written into stories
and songs and poems. Stories plastered on the walls,
songs sticking to the lampshades
and poems laying on pillows.

On Monday morning Pearl **scooted** off to school.

And she spoke!

Not just with one word, but with sentences, long, extravagant sentences.

When Pearl's teacher said, "Name an adjective,"

Pearl cried, "It's too hard to name just one. . . ."

hot
&
cold

old
&
young

sweet & sour

light & HEAVY

smooth &
LUMPY

shy &
BOLD

LOOSE
&
tight

black & white

When Jack asked her what she had for lunch, Pearl said,

"I have a sandwich. . . .

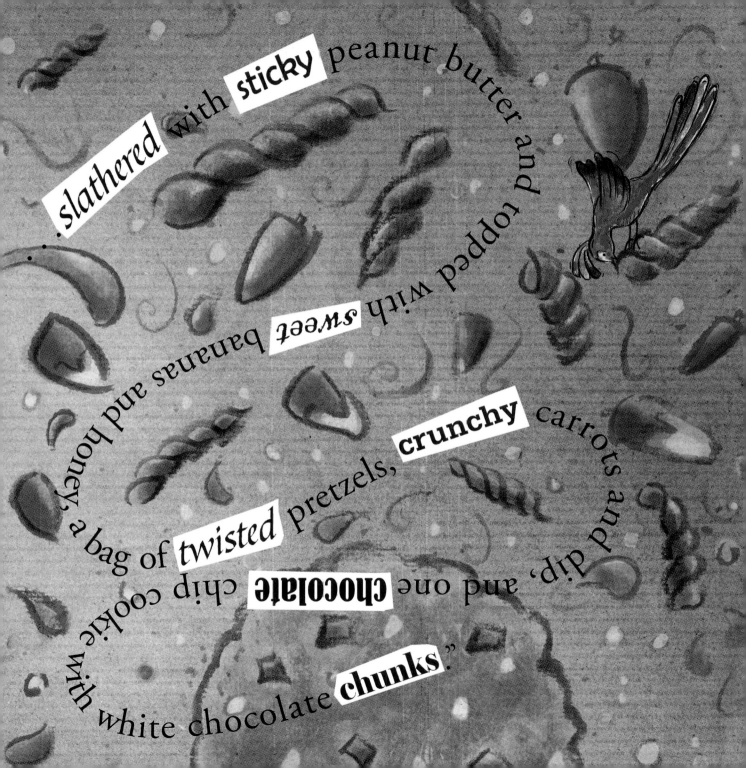

slathered with **sticky** peanut butter and topped with *sweet* bananas and honey, a bag of *twisted* pretzels, **crunchy** carrots and dip, and one **chocolate** chip cookie with white chocolate **chunks**."

And when Molly gave Pearl a pink journal,
Pearl's words *flowed*.

They flowed like lemonade
from a pitcher,
pink and
sweet.

She wrote

and **wrote**

and wrote!

Wow

miracle

SCARIES   interesting

Imagine   Celebrations   CRANBERR

Magic   *flawless*

JUMPING

Pearls

ACTION!   RHAPSODY

Funky   ORIGINS

GINGER

And Pearl thought to herself,
no more word troubles for me, I'm Pearl . . .

Pearl the Word Girl!